MY NOTES ....by MR Chicken

In Italian - ROME is called ROMA.

I must see ...The COLOSSEUM. The Pantheon, the FORUM and Spanish Steps, the Vatican and THE MOUTH OF TRUTH - Legend has it that if you put your wing in the mouth and tell a fib it will bite it.
- THIS SOUNDS EXCITING!

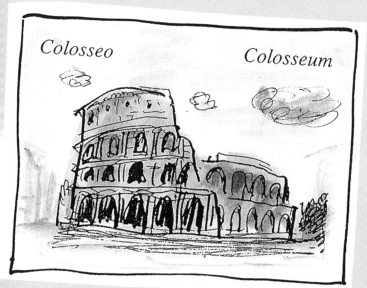

Colosseo          Colosseum

Basilica di San Pietro     St. Peter's Basilica

THIS BOOK BELONGS TO

D0875987

# Mr Chicken arriva a

# ROMA

## (Mr Chicken arrives in Rome)

## Leigh HOBBS

ALLEN&UNWIN

SYDNEY • MELBOURNE • AUCKLAND • LONDON

*For my sister, Jenny*

First published by Allen & Unwin in 2016

Allen & Unwin – Australia
83 Alexander Street, Crows Nest NSW 2065, Australia
Phone: (61 2) 8425 0100
Email: info@allenandunwin.com
Web: www.allenandunwin.com

Allen & Unwin – UK
Ormond House, 26–27 Boswell Street,
London WC1N 3JZ, UK
Phone: +44 (0) 20 8785 5995
Email: info@murdochbooks.co.uk
Web: www.murdochbooks.co.uk

A Cataloguing-in-Publication entry is available from the
National Library of Australia: www.trove.nla.gov.au.
A catalogue record for this book is available from the British Library.

ISBN (AUS) 978 1 925266 77 1
ISBN (UK) 978 1 74336 875 6

Cover design by Leigh Hobbs and Sandra Nobes
Text design by Sandra Nobes
Typeset in Cochin by Sandra Nobes
Colour reproduction by Splitting Image, Clayton, Victoria
This book was printed in May 2016 at Hang Tai Printing (Guang Dong) Ltd., China.

1 3 5 7 9 10 8 6 4 2

**www.leighhobbs.com**

Thanks to my Roman friend, Federica De Vito, who showed me where to get the best gelato in Rome.
And many thanks as always to Team Chicken: Erica Wagner, Elise Jones and Sandra Nobes.

Even as a baby, Mr Chicken
was different to other boys and girls.
Instead of playing games, he dreamt
about life in Ancient Rome.

Now he was a grown-up and off
to Rome on his first ever visit.

Mr Chicken was flying business class, for the fine food and extra leg room.

Just before landing, he caught a glimpse of his first Roman ruin. 'Magnifico!' he cried.

Mr Chicken arrived in
Rome incognito and all excited.
He'd hired a guide named Federica to show
him some ruins and help him meet some real Romans.

'Buongiorno, Signor Pollo,' called Federica,
recognising Mr Chicken straight away. 'Welcome to Rome.'

'Climb aboard my Vespa,' she said, 'and hold on to your hat.'
Mr Chicken did what he was told and off they went.
His childhood dream was about to begin.

Soon they were in the middle of Rome, crossing
Piazza Venezia. 'Look,' said Federica. 'Il Colosseo.'
Mr Chicken couldn't wait to get
up close and touch it…

COLOSSEO

COLOSSEUM

…and when he did, he took a photo to prove that he had been there.
'Of course, there is more to Rome than just the ruins,'
said Federica. 'Now you must taste Italian ice-cream.'

'We call it gelato. There are lots of flavours: cocco, caffè, cassata, melone and menta, pesca and fragola. And that's just a few.'

'Mmmm. Delicioso,' said Mr Chicken, licking his lips.

The Roman tour
continued, with
Mr Chicken doing
his best to remember
his manners.

Federica parked outside the Pantheon so Signor Pollo
could take a picture. But there wasn't time to dawdle
for there was much she wished to show him ...

...like the Vatican, where she and Mr Chicken joined the crowd, all waiting to see the Pope.

However, Mr Chicken
was hot and hungry.

So Federica took him
to the Trevi Fountain
for a dip before lunch.
Soon Mr Chicken had
a big decision to make.

Would he have spaghetti or cannelloni, penne or tortellini?
Or maybe even pasta alla papalina?

Mr Chicken studied the menu and chose the tagliatelle.

Next, after a quick stop by the river Tiber,
Federica left him at a church.
'Join the queue while I arrange a treat for tonight,'
she said. 'I'll collect you later.'

Mr Chicken lined up as instructed, put a wing in the Mouth of Truth and waited.

After all that sightseeing he needed a nap…which turned into a deep sleep.

Suddenly, Mr Chicken was back in Ancient Rome.
He was an emperor in a toga making speeches,
and a guest of honour being fanned at a feast.
His face and big bottom were on coins...

...and statues
and pots.
Even a table!

Everywhere Mr Chicken went in his chariot,
Romans cheered.

Then this lovely dream turned into a nasty nightmare.

Mr Chicken was all alone in the Colosseum with a hungry monster.

And then, when he was chased by gladiators waving their tridents,
it looked like Mr Chicken's trip to Rome was in ruins.

That is, until he heard, 'Wake up, Signor Pollo! Wake up!'
It was Federica, back with her Vespa.

'Enough rest,' she said. 'It's time for my surprise.
Would you like to drive?'

Federica held on to Mr Chicken's hat with one hand
and pointed directions with the other.

Mr Chicken didn't know it yet,
but Federica's family was having him for dinner.

He was the guest of honour.

'Meet my family,' said Federica. 'Viola, Romano, Lucia and Cristina.
My mother Anna, Luca my father, and sister Alessia.'

'Buonasera!' said Mr Chicken, proud to have perfected his pronunciation.

In between eating, Mr Chicken told tales about
his thrilling travels and learnt a little about Federica's family.
How lovely it was to meet and eat with a real Roman
family. But all too soon it was time to say goodbye.

On the way to the airport,
Mr Chicken had a last lick
of his favourite flavour.

Then, with a 'Ciao' and a peck on both cheeks, his day in Rome was over. 'I've never met anyone like you, Signor Pollo,' said Federica. 'Grazie,' said Mr Chicken. 'Arrivederci.'

Back in the air, Mr Chicken spread his wings and put
his feet up. He'd seen ruins and met some Romans.
Best of all, he'd made some real Roman friends.

Piazza del Popolo

At the Vatican

Lunch near the Trevi Fountain

In the Trevi Fountain

# MY ROMAN

The Forum

Going up the Spanish Steps

Mouth of Truth ↑

The Pantheon

The Forum (still)

By the Tiber →